Written by Tom Paxton   Illustrated by Don Vanderbeek

 ScottForesman

A Division of HarperCollins*Publishers*

Engelbert is big and gray.

On sunny days he likes to play.

He has friends of every size. . .

lions, monkeys, bats, and flies.

When the summer sun is hot,

they all meet at a favorite spot.

Engelbert's friends play on a
tower, and Engelbert gives them
a nice, cool shower.